THE WILDERNESS

OH! AND LET'S NOT FORGET OKTOBER.

STEVE MᶜCARTHY

PAPA EVEREST

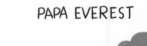

WALKER BOOKS
AND SUBSIDIARIES

LONDON • BOSTON • SYDNEY • AUCKLAND

First published 2022 by Walker Books Ltd, 87 Vauxhall Walk, London SE11 5HJ
Text & Illustrations © 2022 Steve McCarthy • The right of Steve McCarthy to be
identified as author and illustrator of this work has been asserted in accordance with
the Copyright, Designs and Patents Act 1988 • This book has been typeset in Futura
T Printed in China • All rights reserved. No part of this book may be reproduced,
transmitted or stored in an information retrieval system in any form or by any means,
graphic, electronic or mechanical, including photocopying, taping and recording,
without prior written permission from the publisher. British Library Cataloguing
in Publication Data: a catalogue record for this book is available from the British
Library • ISBN 978-1-4063-8519-9 • www.walker.co.uk • 10 9 8 7 6 5 4 3 2 1

Well now, dear reader, let me introduce you to the very impressive Vasylenko family.

Just like every other day, the Vasylenko family braved the wild, looking for adventure.

And just like every other day ...
Oktober stayed in.

Much like his brothers and sisters, Oktober dreamed of being a great adventurer.

But, unlike them, Oktober went on his adventures inside books, safe from the climby, slimy, grimy, wet, cold and wild outside.

"Are you reading *101 Ways to Avoid Getting Lost in the Wild?*" said January.

"No! That was yesterday, this is *102 Ways to Avoid Getting Eaten,*" said Oktober.

The Vasylenkos dreamed
of wild things, and wild places,
and all the wild adventures
they would have.

But Oktober couldn't sleep.
He was thinking of the wildest thing of all,
in the wildest place of all, a monster called
'The Wilderness' that lurks...

"Outside?!" yelled Oktober.
"I don't want to go outside!
Into the wilderness, where the wilderness is,
where The Wilderness *lives!*"

"The wilderness isn't a monster. That's just
a silly thing people say," said Dad.

"I heard it *is* a monster," said May.
"And it smooshes children,
    eats rocks, rides motorbikes,
    and maybe it could
    be my sidekick!"

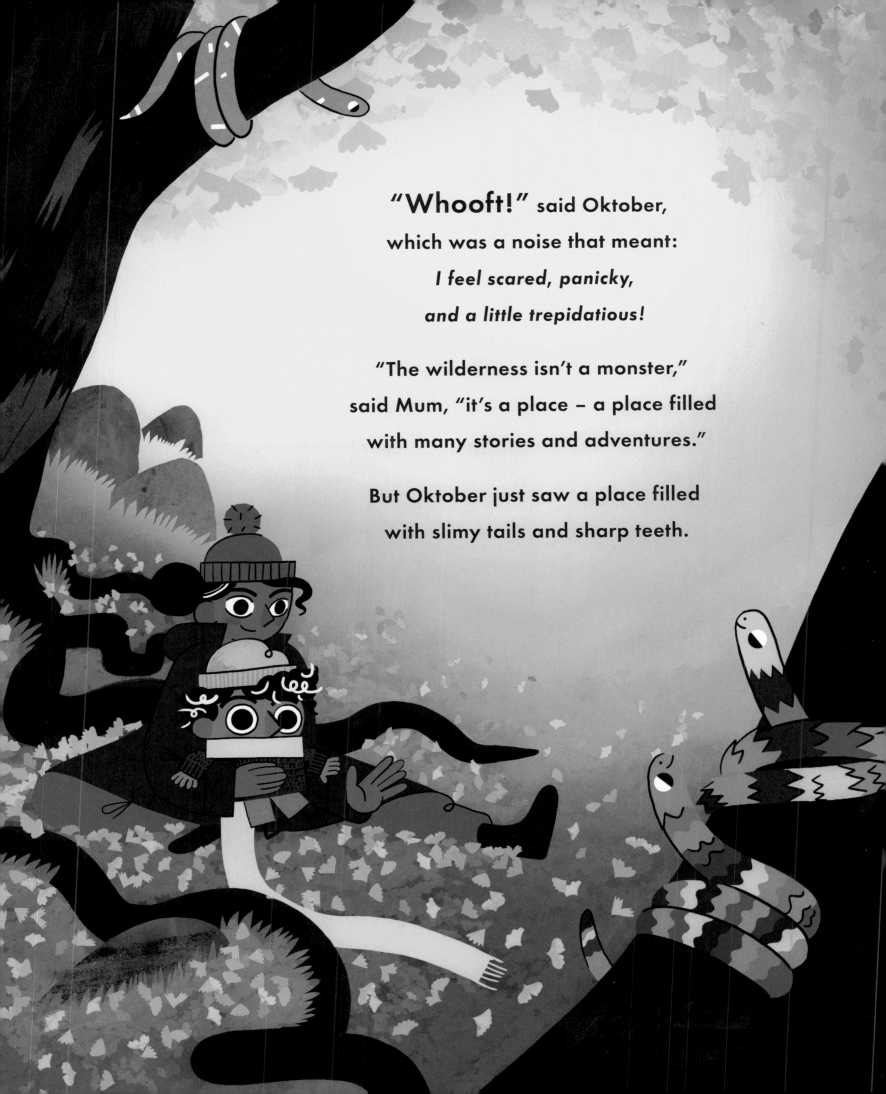

"Whooft!" said Oktober,
which was a noise that meant:
*I feel scared, panicky,
and a little trepidatious!*

"The wilderness isn't a monster,"
said Mum, "it's a place – a place filled
with many stories and adventures."

But Oktober just saw a place filled
with slimy tails and sharp teeth.

"What if The Wilderness is down there..." said Oktober.

"It's OK to be scared," said Dad. "I get scared, too.

Scared is how you *feel*, but bravery is what you *do*,

so let's do this together and be twice as brave."

"What if The Wilderness is up there..." said Oktober.

"We don't know what we'll see and not knowing things
can be scary," said Mum. "But let's find out together,
and the more we know, the less scary things will be."

"**Whooft!**" said Mum, which was a noise that meant:

I feel happy, glad, and a little wonderstruck!

"I can see treasures! All the way home!" said August.

But Oktober didn't see treasures. He saw a murky
mist, hiding hideous creatures, and 142 things
in the wild that leave a very itchy rash.

I'll never be brave enough to be an adventurer, he thought.
Can't they see that?

Now, listen, dear reader,

yes – I'm talking to you!

Pay close attention.

Stick together

and keep your wits about you,

because if we lose each other, we might just get ...

It was at this moment, as Oktober tumbled
towards certain death, that for some strange reason
he remembered ... it was actually *143* things in the
wild that can give you a very itchy rash.

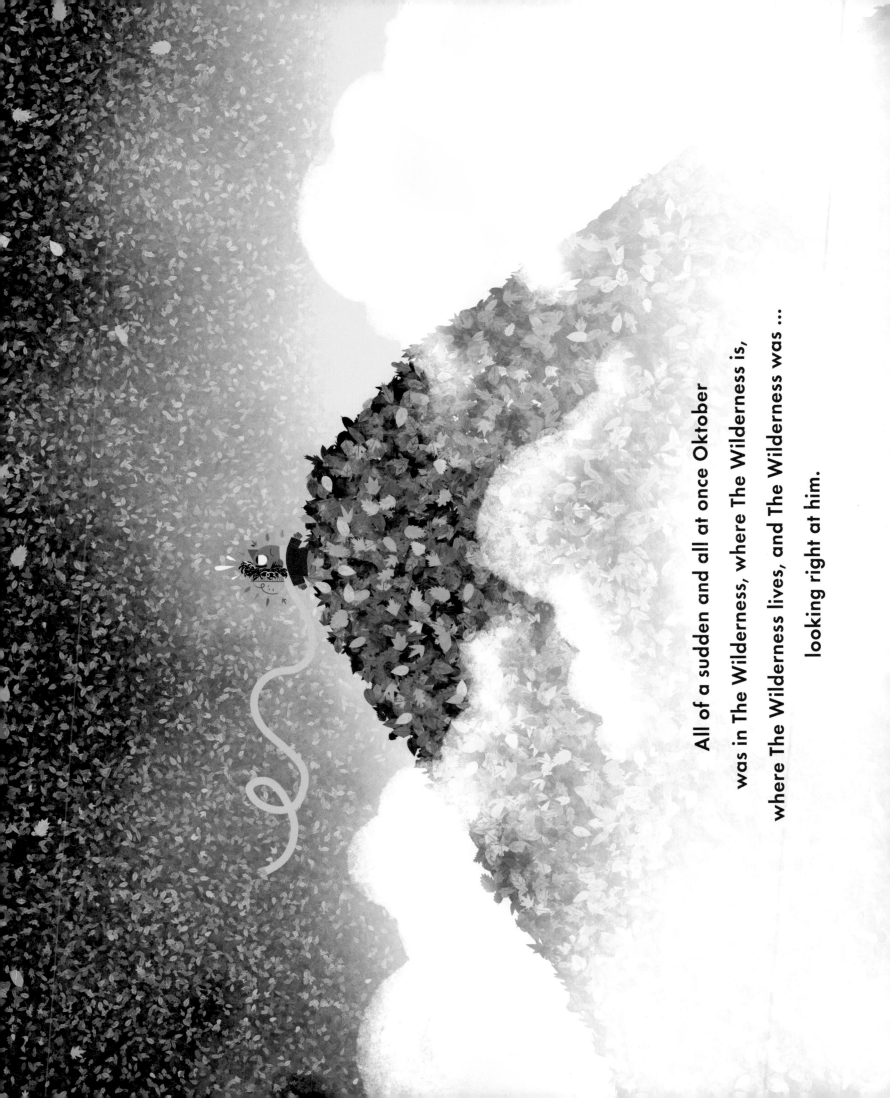

All of a sudden and all at once Oktober

was in The Wilderness, where The Wilderness is,

where The Wilderness lives, and The Wilderness was ...

looking right at him.

But as The Wilderness whooshed into a terrible tornado,
Oktober realized something.

The Wilderness wasn't a monster,
they were ... scared.

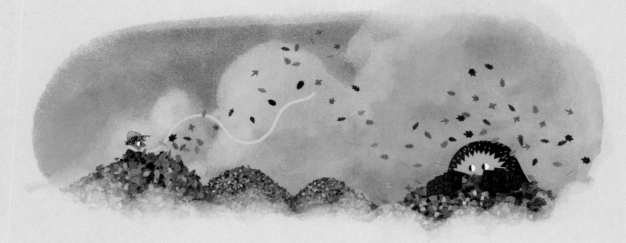

Oktober knew because Oktober was scared too.
So he did something brave.

He waved.

And to his surprise,
The Wilderness waved back.

"**Whooft!**" said The Wilderness, which was
a noise that meant: *I feel happy, a bit
scared, and a little wonderstruck!*

"You must be lost?" they said.

"How did you know?" said Oktober.

"Well, I go where the wind takes me," said The Wilderness.
"And I never know where I'll be, so it takes someone
getting lost to find me."

"I'm trying to find my way home," said Oktober.

"Well," said The Wilderness, "maybe you just need to
see where you've been, from a different point of view."

Oktober could see above the clouds, he could see wild places,
filled with wild things, and in the middle of it all – a house!

"That's where my home is! Where we Vasylenkos live!"

"I can take you there," said The Wilderness.

With The Wilderness by his side,
Oktober saw all the things he had seen before,
only now he saw them differently.

He saw wild things on their own adventures

and he saw the wild places where they live.

And he saw Mum and Dad,

who saw a brave little adventurer returning home ...

and Oktober saw this, too.

"GOOD TO MEET YOU!"

Just like every other day,
the whole Vasylenko family braved
the wild, looking for adventure.

But on this particular day, dear reader,
Oktober decided to write his own adventure book,
and he called this book, *The Wilderness*.

EXPLODING MUSHROOM
Detonates when embarrassed

RUNNING ROOT
Top speed 42 mph

TOUCH-ME-NOT
Not good at parties

HAMMER PLANT
Careful around your toes

BOOHOO BAMBOO
Likes sad music

SNEEZEWORT
Allergic to children

BUZZ BUTTONS
Causes numb tongue(s)